✳ THE ARRIVAL ✳

Shaun Tan

h
Hodder
Children's
Books

I

───────❦───────

for my parents

First published in 2006 by Lothian Children's Books
This edition published in 2007 by Hodder Children's Books

Text and illustrations copyright © Shaun Tan 2006
www.shauntan.net

Hodder Children's Books,
338 Euston Road, London NW1 3BH
Hodder Children's Books Australia,
Level 17/207, Kent Street, Sydney, NSW 2000

The right of Shaun Tan to be identified as the author,
and illustrator of this Work has been asserted by him in
accordance with the Copyright, Designs and Patents Act 1988

INSPECTION

ISBN: 978 0 340 96993 9
10 9

Printed in China

Hodder Children's Books is a division of Hachette Children's Books
An Hachette UK Company
www.hachette.co.uk

Illustration media: *Graphite pencil on paper, digitally coloured*
Design by *Shaun Tan*
Prepress by *Hell Colour Australia*
Printed in China by *C&C Offset Printing*

Australia Council
for the Arts

This project has been assisted by
the Australian Government through
the Australia Council, its arts fundi...
and advisory body.

29

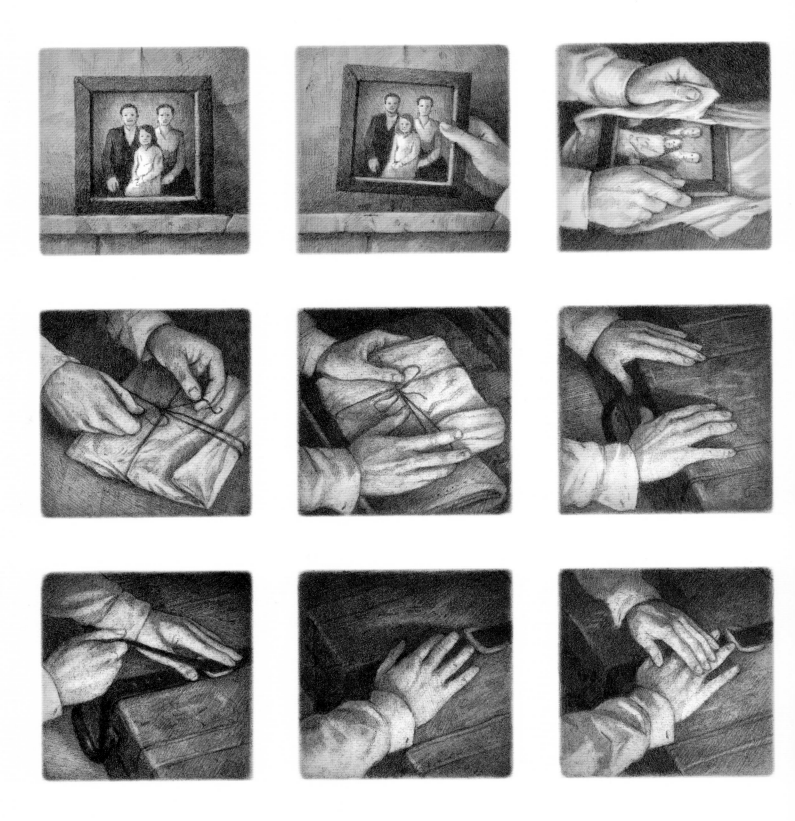

II

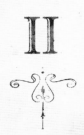

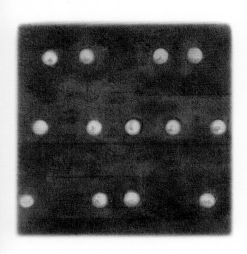  

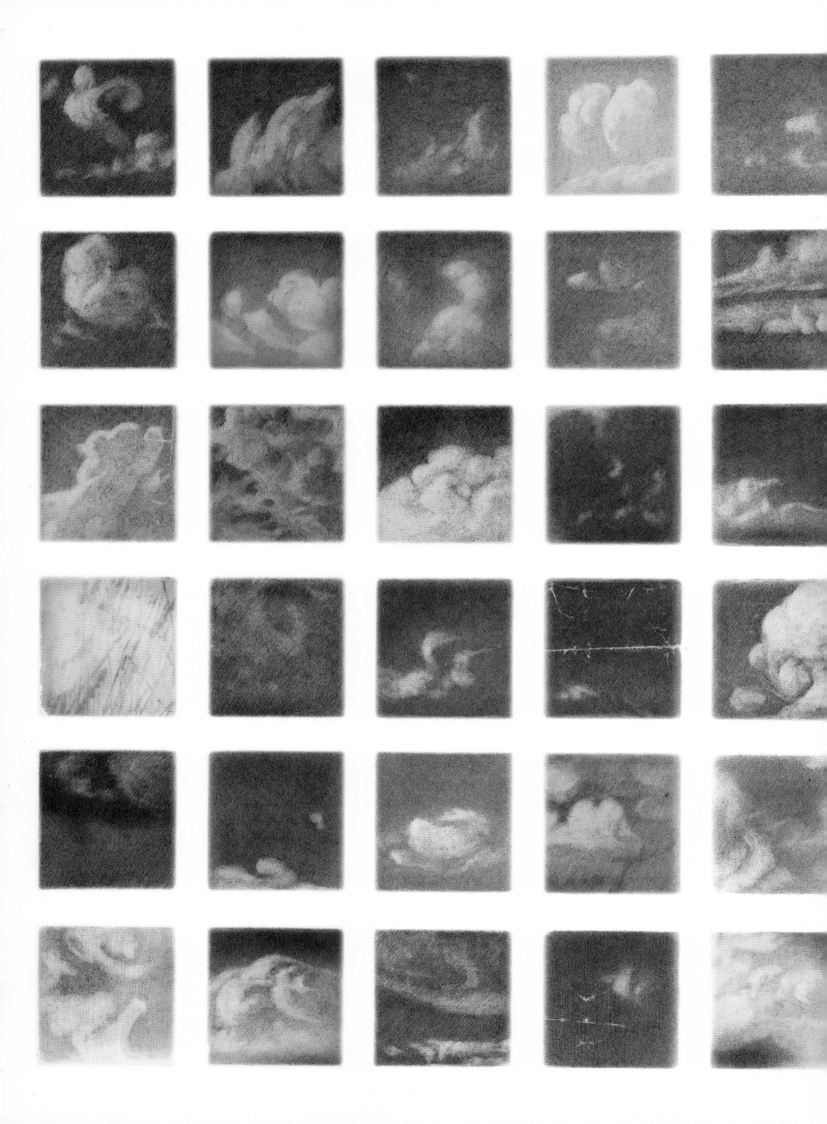

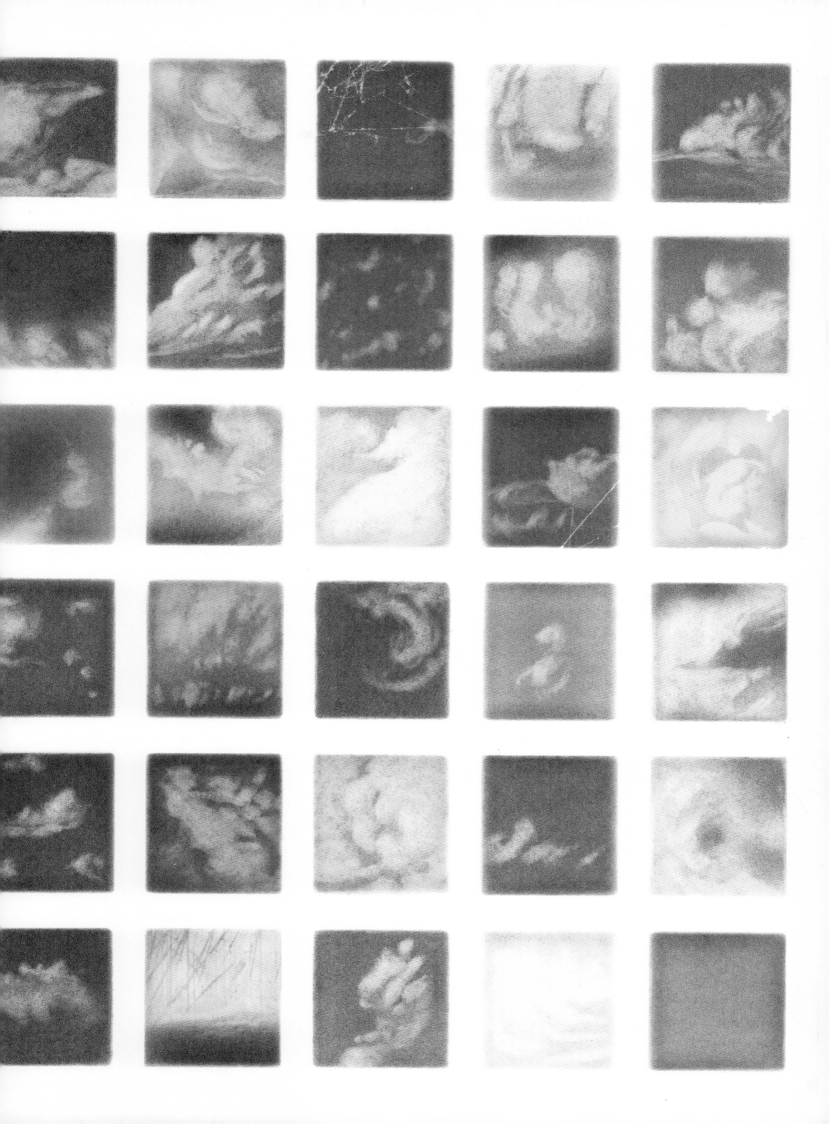

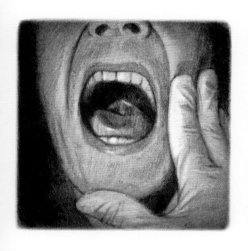

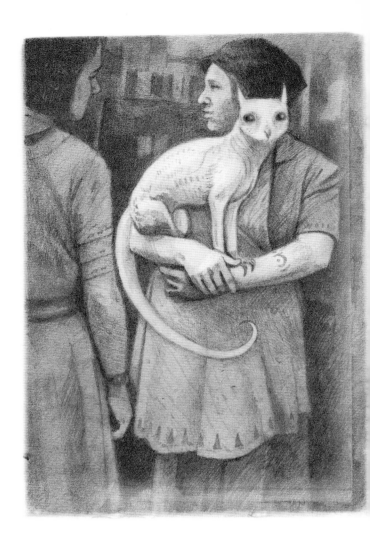

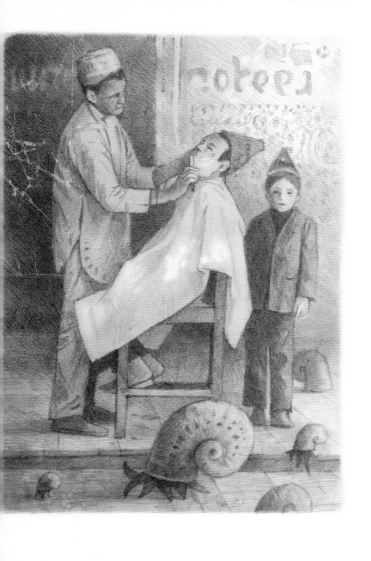

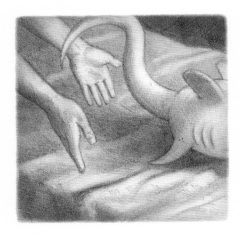

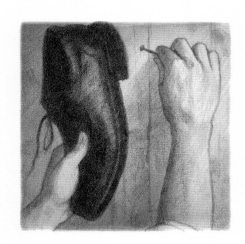

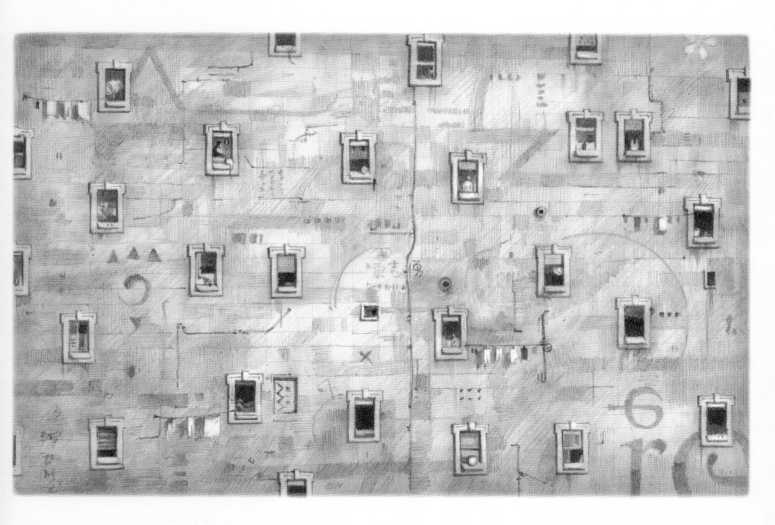

III

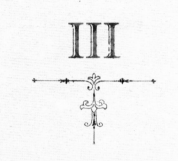

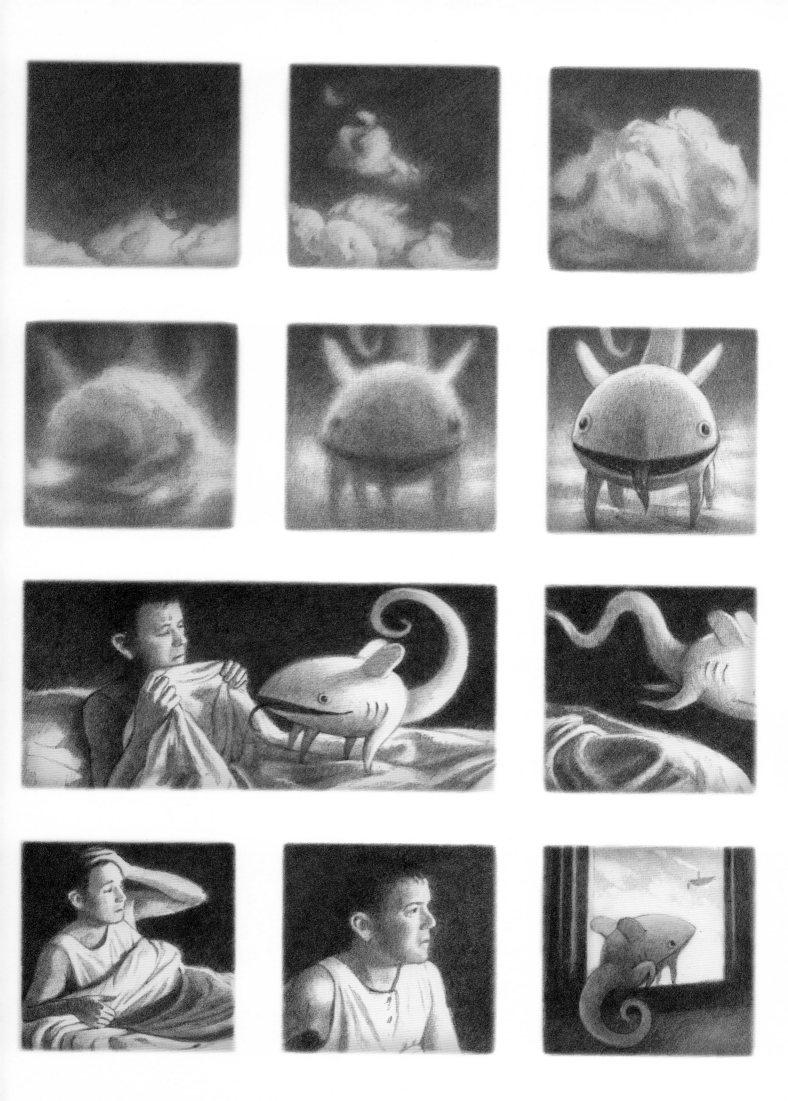

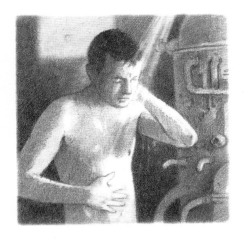

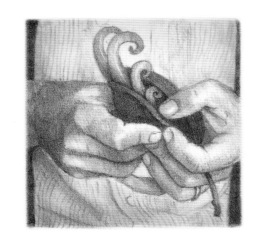

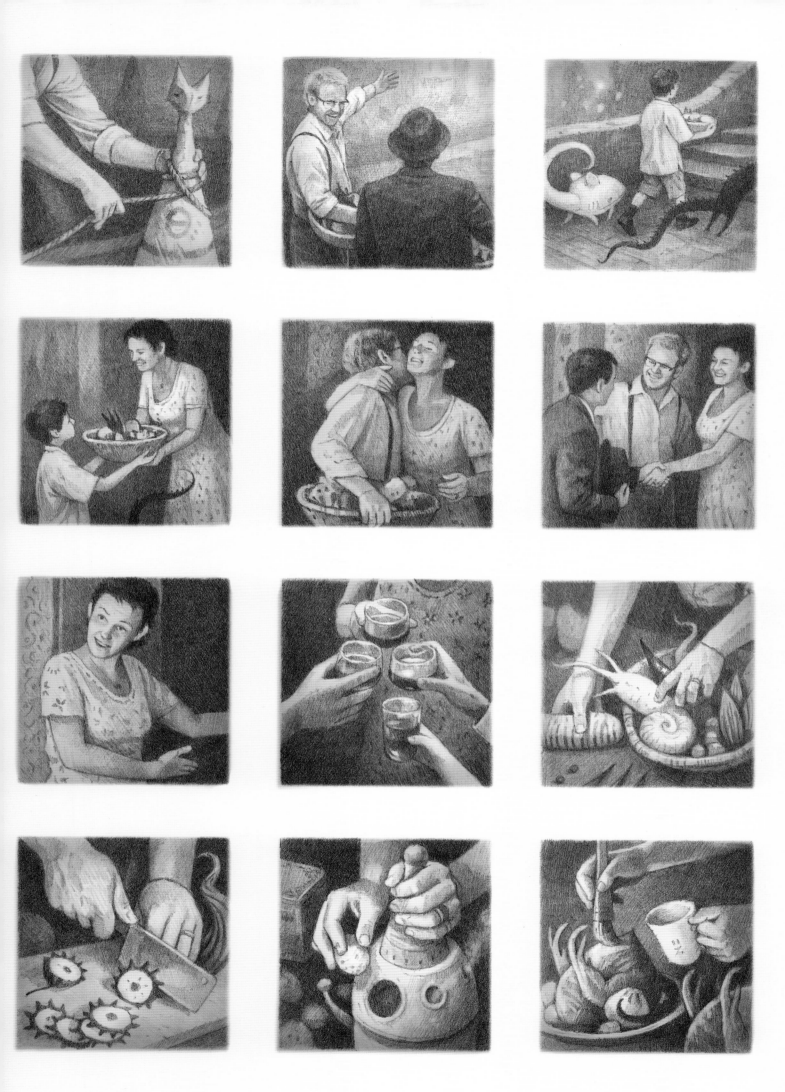

IV

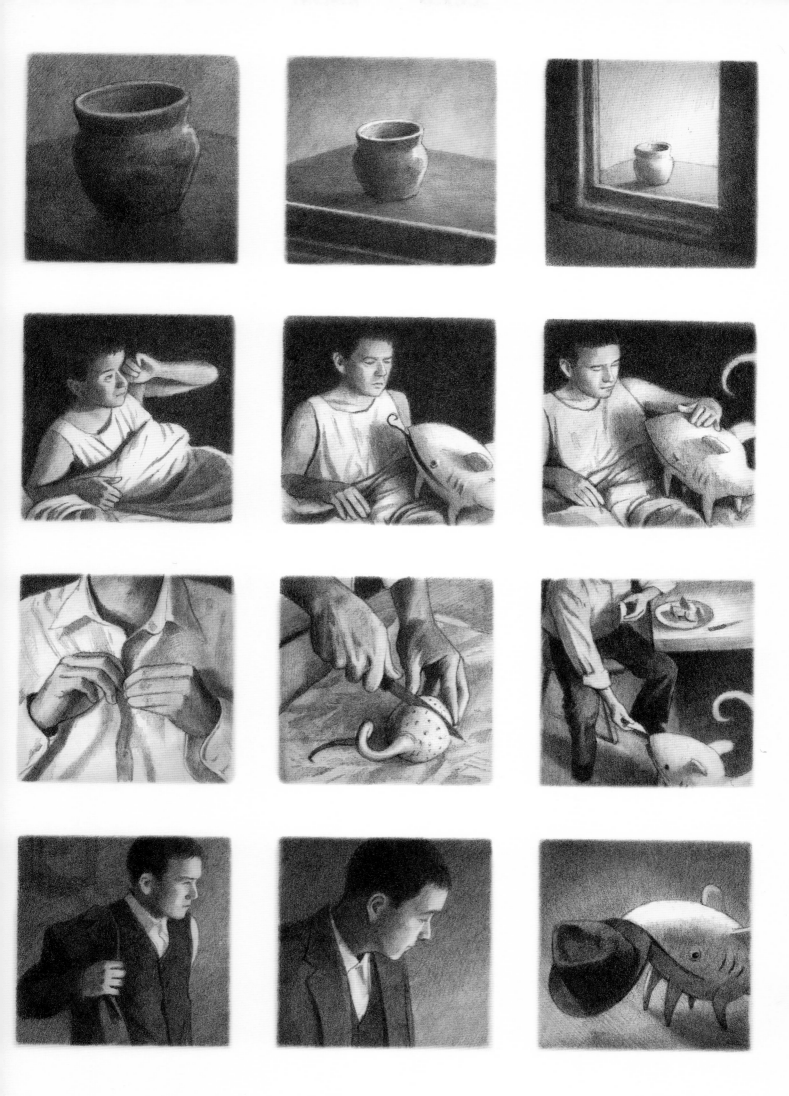

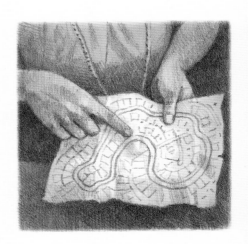

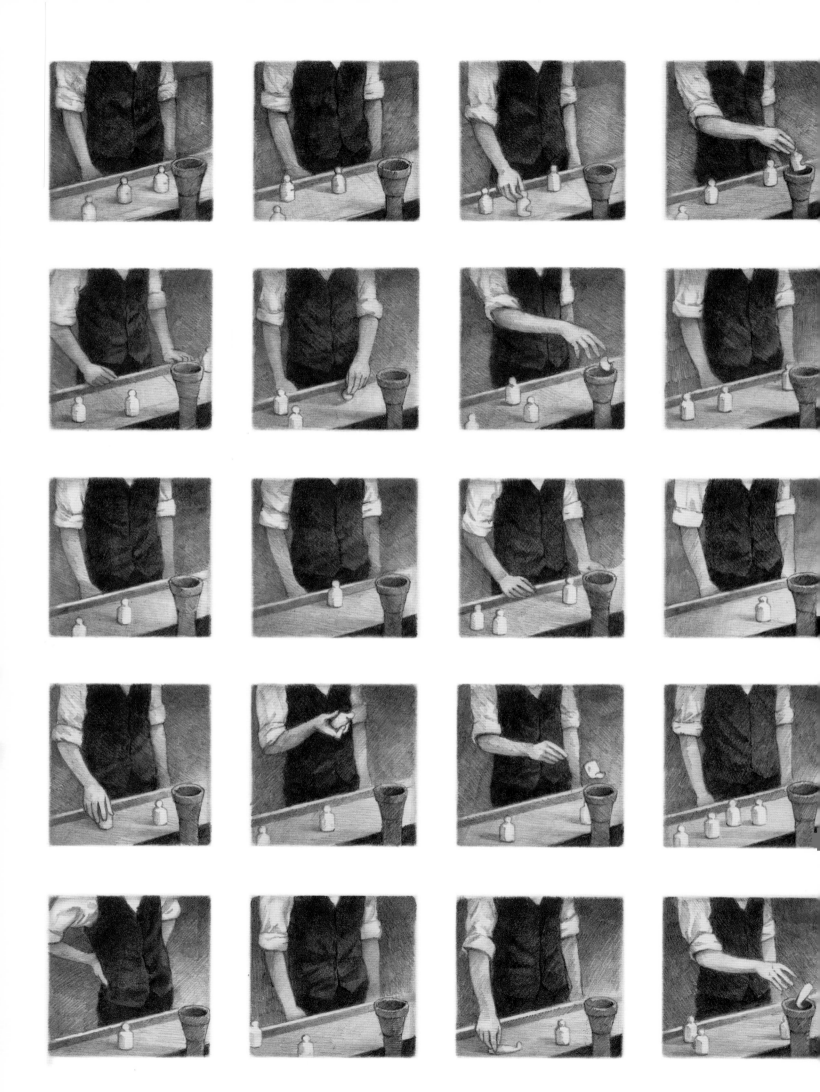

V

VI

Artist's Note

I am grateful to the following people for their assistance during the four years of research, development, and drawing that went into this book; my parents Bing and Christine Tan, Paul Tan, Helen Chamberlin, Sophie Byrne, Amanda Verschuren, Susan Marie, Rachel Marie, Simon Clarke, Deanna Cooney, Sophia Witte and Sarah Weaving, Zacharie Evers, Philip Evers and Kirsten Schweder, David Yeates and Kathryn Robinson, Karen Kennedy and the Bold Park Community School, Jeremy Reston, Nick Stathopoulos, the Ruffo family, everyone at the Fremantle Children's Literature Centre, Christobel Bennett at Subiaco Museum, Will Lauria, Peter Lothian, Tina Denham, Anna Dalziel and all the staff at Lothian Books for their ongoing faith – and patience! My greatest appreciation goes of course to my partner Inari Kiuru for all her support, advice and encouragement. Special thanks go to Diego the parrot for inspiring most of the creatures in this book.

Thanks also to the Australia Council, The State Library of Western Australia, Inglewood Public Library, the Town of Vincent Public Library and the National Maritime Museum in Sydney. Much of this book was inspired by anecdotal stories told by migrants of many different countries and historical periods, including my father who came to Western Australia from Malaysia in 1960. Two important references were *The Immigrants* by Wendy Lowenstein and Morag Loh (Hyland House, 1977), and *Tales from a Suitcase* by Will Davies and Andrea Dal Bosco (Lothian Books, 2001) – many thanks to all those who described their journeys and impressions in these books. The drawing of migrants on a ship pays homage to a painting by Tom Roberts, *Going South*, 1886, at the National Gallery of Victoria, Melbourne. Other visual references and inspirations include a 1912 photograph of a newsboy announcing the Titanic sinking, picture postcards of New York from the turn of the century, photographs of street scenes from post-war Europe, Vittorio De Sica's 1948 film 'Bicycle Thieves' and Gustav Dore's engraving 'Over London by Rail' c. 1870. Several drawings of immigrant processing, passport pictures and the 'arrival hall' are based on photographs taken at Ellis Island, New York from 1892 to 1954, many of which can be found in the collection of the Ellis Island Immigration Museum. For further comment, please visit www.shauntan.net

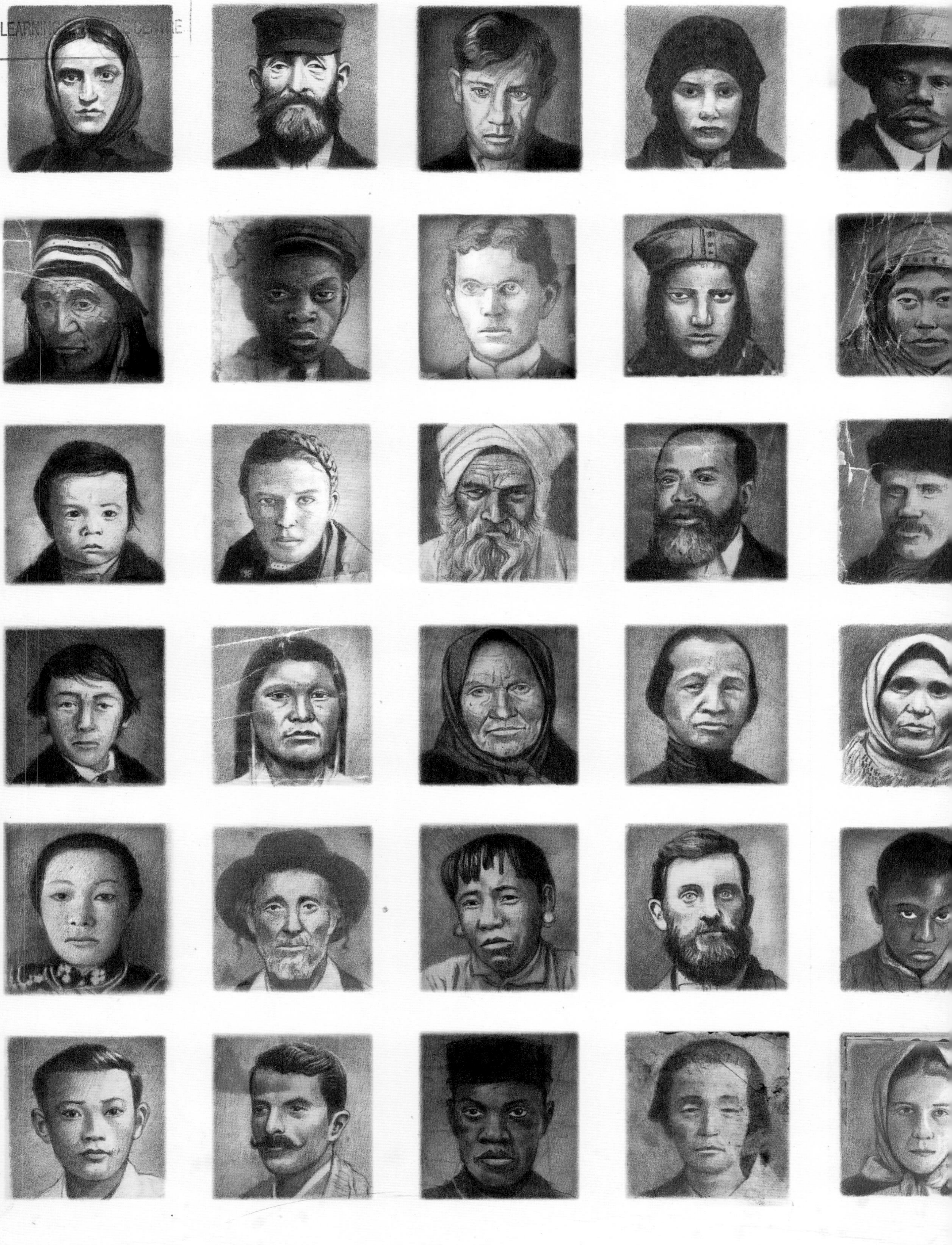